THE COLORFUL SNOWMAN

♥ To Chris, Dylan and Cassia:
Thank you for your encouragement and support along this
journey and for making my world more colorful every day.

And to all of my fellow teachers: Our job has become
fiercely challenging in the last few years.
Keep loving your littles and looking for the special moments.
Hopefully reading this book together will be one of them. - KP

One cold winter morning,
the children of Cranberry Street
woke up to see that it had snowed…

AGAIN!!!

EVERYTHING was covered in snow.
The trees were white. The streets were
white. The cars were white.

Everything was white!

"This street needs more color,"
said Christopher and Anne,
so they grabbed their paints
and ran outside.

A few hours later,
they looked at their work.
They were so proud.
A colorful snowman!

Just then, the other children
came outside to play.
They didn't like the Colorful Snowman.

"That's NOT a snowman,"
said one of the children.
"Snowmen are NOT colorful!"
declared another.
The children started to laugh.

Christopher and Anne
looked at each other and said,
"He IS a snowman!!!

He may not look like all the other
snowmen you have seen,
but he IS made of snow.
Every snowman can be different.

A snowman could have rocks for eyes...

OR he could have tennis balls.

He could even have chocolate chip
cookie eyes, but you wouldn't call him
a chocolate chip cookie man.
He's a snowman!

A snowman could have a carrot for a nose…

OR he could have a pickle.

He could even have a hot dog nose,
but you wouldn't call him a hot dog man.
He's a snowman!

A snowman
could have
sticks for arms...

OR he could
have brooms.

He could even have toilet plungers
for arms, but you wouldn't call him
a toilet plunger man.
He's a snowman!

A snowman
could have
a winter hat
on his head...

OR he could
have a bucket.

He could even have underwear
on his head, but you wouldn't
call him an underwear man.
He's a snowman!

A snowman can even be
colorful like ours!
Being different is
what makes us special!"

The children walked away thinking
about what they had heard.

The next morning,
they got to work.

The snowmen of Cranberry Street
had NEVER looked better.

Made in the USA
Middletown, DE
07 January 2024